ONE
EXTR★
ORDINARY
DAY

ONE
EXTR★
ORDINARY
DAY

one encounter
will change
everything

Tyndale House Publishers, Inc.
Carol Stream, Illinois

HAROLD MYRA

Library of Congress Cataloging-in-Publication Data

Myra, Harold Lawrence, date.
   One extraordinary day / Harold Myra.
      p. cm.
   ISBN-13: 978-1-4143-2358-9
   ISBN-10: 1-4143-2358-1
   1. Spiritual life—Fiction 2. Spiritual direction—Fiction. 3. Angels—Fiction. I. Title.
   PS3563.Y7O54 2008
   813'.54—dc22   2008020383

Printed in the United States of America

14   13   12   11   10   09   08

7   6   5   4   3   2   1

Acknowledgments

Hearty thanks to Ron Beers, Carol Traver, Jon Farrar, and Jeremy Taylor for their encouragement and creative refinements.

AWAKENING

The alarm barely penetrated David's sleep. He fumbled with the unfamiliar hotel clock, found the button, and pressed.

Ten minutes later, another alarm blared at him from across the room. Although he had set it himself, he threw back the covers and stamped toward the sound, slammed it quiet, then burrowed back into his pillow.

An hour later, morning sunlight through the sliding glass door played on his face. He opened one eye. Outside, aspen and birch leaves filtered the light. A swallow flitted by. He sat bolt upright and looked at the clock beside him.

Already 6:30! He had only one day here, and now he had wasted the best hour.

David had wanted to rise before dawn, to inhale these surroundings as the trees and lake became visible. He loved rising at dawn to see the sunrise and feel some control over his day, though he hadn't done so in years. Now the sun was already bright in a blue sky.

He felt little control over his life these days. The communications company where he worked had downsized, firing half his colleagues. Maybe he'd be next.

To make matters worse, he felt betrayed by his boss, Frank, who had persuaded him to give up a very good job to take his current position. Now David realized Frank had known all along that his company was in trouble, that David's strengths would enable him to function with fewer people. It was particularly galling that Frank had lured him not with money but with a mission he knew David believed in—providing hope to mentally ill children. David cared deeply for children and had been willing to swallow a reduced salary. He had accepted the deal but now would have to do the work of at least two people; as a result, he had come to detest Frank.

Twisting his body toward the window and putting his feet on the floor, he reached over to pick up a photo of his wife, Marcia. It was his favorite— she was looking out from under a beach umbrella with an impish grin. At least Marcia wouldn't let him go.

David stood, ran his fingers through his reddish brown hair, pulled his jeans on, and buttoned them over his flat belly, the result of careful eating and no-nonsense workouts. He had always brought passion to whatever he did and drove himself to be self-disciplined and to make a difference in the world. He inserted the coffee bag into the lodge's little Black & Decker coffeemaker and filled the carafe only halfway. Lately he wanted his coffee stronger and stronger. He felt like he had been an ice skater pumping full-bore through life and gaining speed but had suddenly hit a patch of dirt and crashed.

Marcia had reserved this room at the lodge for him. "Get away—at least for one day," she had said. "Go up north this Sunday. Take all day in the woods. Decompress!"

Thank goodness for Marcia. He hated making her feel bad; he wanted to match her enthusiasm for life as he always had. But Frank's treachery and David's own career slump made his drive and dreams of significance seem a farce.

The two mugs of black coffee were just enough to wash down the big sweet roll he had bought the night before. Now he was wired, but he sat quietly, staring at the woods and lake. His parents had often brought him here as a child to explore this lake and the trails through the woods. Now he longed for that uncomplicated joy, for the solitude and wonder of sighting a hawk floating above or being startled by the warning snort of a deer. Once he had come upon a doe in a meadow with two speckled fawns, one nursing at her side. He had scarcely breathed as he watched until the fawn pulled away and all three walked slowly into the woods.

Finally David slid open the glass door and walked down to the lake. At water's edge he watched five seagulls skimming the surface, rising, plunging, soaring in their spontaneous choreography. Two mallards dipped toward the lake and gracefully hit the water.

In that instant, magnificent music erupted into David's world, resonating throughout his body, music of unknown instruments lifting and inspiring. At the same moment he saw the blue sky shattered by a kaleidoscope of colors and vivid images pulsing from horizon to horizon. On the lake, shimmering, cascading light illumined the waves, reflecting purples, magentas, and greens.

A sliver of something like joy rippled through him and then evaporated. Fragrances filled his

nostrils, aromas he found so delightful he involun-
tarily breathed deeply to capture more.

All this happened in a moment and was gone.
The extraordinary phenomenon that was forever
imprinted on his memory was over in a moment,
leaving every sense of his mind and body jolted,
tantalized, drawn into the strange, celebratory
dynamics, as if his entire being were made for
them.

A few years before, David had happened to
look out his window during a storm just as a bolt
of lightning struck a nearby tree. It had sheared off
half the trunk, and David had been stunned at both
the blinding light and the *force*—like a giant sledgehammer of light that had slammed into his yard.

Now, standing at lake's edge, he felt the same
extreme of force, but far more than a sledgehammer
of white light. It had captured the sky with colors
and shapes and had reverberated like cannon fire.
Yet like the lightning hitting the tree, the mysterious
phenomenon was over in seconds. What had it
been? Could it actually have lasted just moments,

all that grandeur, all that force and image and fragrance already vanished?

He looked around. All was as it had been. No broken trees. No breaks in the lake's perimeter. Just clear sunlight shimmering on the waves. He scanned the sky. Only a few white clouds in the expanse of blue. He sniffed the air. Nothing but the scent of pine. He looked behind him to the hotel. No one in sight.

He stood on the sand by the lapping water for long moments, letting all the elements of those extraordinary seconds flow through his consciousness.

As he slowly sat down on a bench, the shapes and sounds and emotions still resonated in his body. He could make no sense of what he had just experienced. He felt like a man on a raft in rapids, plunging and spinning through waves, spray, rocks, and logs, not knowing what might befall him next. At the same time, nibbling at the deep pools of his *angst* was a wondrous elixir of the scents and sounds and images . . . and a tantalizing element of peace.

The mallards flew off. The gulls had settled
across the lake, five white, bobbing specks on the
waves. Yet the serenity around him did nothing
to soothe his inner turmoil. What was happening
to him? He looked down at the white pebbles of
the manicured walk beside his feet. Everything
was perfect, lovely, "decompressing"—yet within
him, a maelstrom of weariness, confusion, and
desires.

David trudged the pebbled walk to the lodge
office, his eyes probing every bush, brick, and
branch. He picked up a fat pinecone and felt its
perfect ridges in his hand. Everything was the same
as when he'd awakened this morning, yet in some
strange way, his world had changed.

In the office he asked the woman at the counter,
"Did you hear that loud sound out at the lake?
About half an hour ago?"

Cocking her head and scrunching her angular
features, the woman looked up from counting
restaurant receipts. "Nope. Didn't." She looked
back down, her fingers still working the receipts.

"It was a strange sound," he said, "and a huge flash of colorful light. Someone must have heard or seen it."

She shrugged.

He watched her moving fingers and squeezed the pinecone till he felt a little stab of pain. "I was hoping someone besides me had heard it."

"Sonic boom!" The hearty voice from behind startled him, and he whirled around to face two older men lounging in captain's chairs. They wore flannel shirts and battered fishing hats.

"Happens up here, young fella," one of them declared. The man was sitting back in his chair, eyes half shut as if to appraise this city boy. His authoritative tone rankled David.

Despite himself, David put a sarcastic edge on his response. "Not a sonic boom. I've heard sonic booms. And there were brilliant, strange lights."

The man edged up in his chair as if savoring this new development. "Strange, eh?" He turned to his companion. "Hear anything or see anything *strange*, Ed?"

Ed, heavyset and sunk in his chair, smiled, shook his head, and said, "Naw, Pete. Not today."

Both men looked at David with amusement. David squeezed the pinecone in his hand so hard he could feel it etching little ridges into his palm. Turning his head toward the woman, David saw she had set aside the receipts, her full attention on the little drama, mouth crinkling toward a smile.

Disdain. The old man's face was eloquent in showing his contempt, with just a trace of triumphant grin. His expression reminded David of an action movie scene he remembered: the hero, with that same look of disdain, had silenced a bragging Nazi youth, staring him into humiliation.

This old guy with the same look was no movie hero. He was pudgy and looked a little like David's boss. In fact, the man reminded David far too much of Frank, and he felt rage growing in his chest. He thought of all sorts of cutting responses, yet he sensed more verbal jousting would most likely result in his being humiliated even more.

David looked over at the woman at the desk.

Her smile masked a hint of gloating satisfaction. She slightly raised her eyebrows as his eyes met hers and then, maddeningly, she winked at him.

Instead of responding, he turned abruptly and stepped outside. Halfway back to the lodge, he flung the pinecone in a high arc toward the lake.

LONGING

Am I going crazy? David asked himself. In his room he fiddled with the TV remote, emotions churning, thoughts darting like sparrows into tangled branches. He had been stunned and confused by that momentary split in the sky with its heralding sounds and scents, but at the same time he had been filled with sweet longings he wanted to feel again. Yet what he felt now was an uncharacteristic rage toward Frank and those two old men and the woman.

This was decidedly unlike David. He was a reader, a thinker, a man with a passion for making a positive difference in the world. In college he had been torn between becoming a literature or history major. He had finally decided on literature; he loved authors ranging from Browning and Tolstoy to Hemingway. Yet he still read history, drawing intense inspiration from towering figures like Washington, Lee, both Roosevelts, and Churchill. He was determined to make strategic contributions as they had. Now, events had stymied him.

Decompress. Marcia had said to decompress. David booted up his laptop and scanned the headlines. Flooding in Bangladesh—thousands homeless. Senator convicted of bribery. Car bomb in a Middle Eastern market killed seventy people. Family murdered in Kansas. Baseball scores. Weather.

He clicked to e-mail. Marcia had sent a smile

greeting with photos. A 20-percent-off coupon from a bookstore. Office messages. He snapped the laptop shut.

The red button on the remote brought the TV screen to life. A woman in a drama accusing a man of infidelity. *Click.* Little children singing beside tall scarecrow puppets. *Click.* A man in rags standing in his devastated home. *Click.* Vintage photos of the Wright brothers in their bicycle shop. *Click.* Protesters screaming in Pakistan. *Click.* A crowd of Middle Eastern mourners carrying a casket through the streets. *Click. Click. Click.*

This wasn't decompression. He pulled the TV furniture forward, reached down for the plug, and yanked it from the wall.

He stared at Marcia's picture, studying her face, so often a source of strength and love and a sense that at the core of his life, all was well. But at this moment, all he felt was depression.

Across the room, he sank into a soft chair and picked up a book he had bought last week. Inspirational poetry with photos of soaring eagles and colorful songbirds. He flipped the pages, trying to engage, then gave up and put it down.

A Gideon Bible was on the table. Never religious, David had always respected the book as literature, and he opened it at the center but then, almost as quickly, snapped it shut as he had the laptop.

Outside, sunlight brightened the trees. A pair of wrens chased each other through the aspens. He watched them fly off and studied the aspen leaves quivering green in the breeze.

The click of the digital clock drew his eyes toward the dead TV screen. Brain scans. As he stared at the gray-green screen, images of brain scans from illustrated articles flowed through his own brain. Red in one part of the brain and blue here and yellow there showing . . . what? He couldn't remember. Red for activity, maybe; yellow for sluggish and dull; blue for who knew what—all this research revealing all kinds of things about the brain, but for what purpose? He felt his own brain at the moment was chaotic red and yellow and blue and chartreuse or whatever colors were jangling together in his mind like dribbled paint on a Jackson Pollock canvas.

David had always sought meaning through purposeful analysis and then action, and now he reached for his running shoes.

On the trails he sprinted, trying to make some sense out of his life. He sped past majestic bur oaks and birch saplings and tall evergreens, for once oblivious to their beauty. He ran in bursts of speed and then walked fast until he came to a bench on the trail. Breathing hard, he slumped down on it.

With the motion came the unexpected. A slight whiff of the mysterious fragrance, the same scent from the phenomenon at the lake.

It electrified all his senses. *What was that?*

He felt he was experiencing the lake phenomenon all over again, every nerve ending suddenly alive in anticipation. His emotions churned with longing. He had no idea what it was he longed for, but the longing was as palpable as fear, or exuberance at a football game, and somehow a crazy mixture of both.

Yet everything was normal. Here he sat. Trees. Trail. A squirrel rustling the leaves. Nothing that could say his fevered brain wasn't pickled with whatever insanities put people into white straitjackets.

Last Christmas he had opened a large, padded envelope. Turned out it was under pressure, and the moment air escaped, so did hundreds of stars and shapes of all colors, flying into the room and sparkling all over the carpet. Like that surprise package—but far, far greater—the phenomenon at the lake had exploded on him, sounds and sights and scents rushing at him and through him.

Was he going crazy? What might scans reveal about his brain and his mind? He forced a smile at an attempt at humor: Ah, the scientist explains! "Here, gentlemen, is the red, spreading all over his medulla—or whatever that oblong thing is—and it's reducing his functioning into absurdity. All this patient needs now is a quick lobotomy."

David's smile died away as he started walking back toward the lake. He didn't want to deny the strange longings he felt, for they were sweet and as wondrous and alluring as the gulls in choreography or the white birches gracing the green shore. Yet when someone longed for food or rest or love, the object of the longing was clear. But this longing— what was it for?

He stooped at the lake's edge to find some flat stones. Gathering several along the shore, he dropped a pile of them at his feet and bent low to skip one across the surface. And another, and another. He counted the number of skips for each stone—seven, eight, even nine or more, depending on the stillness of the water's surface and the stone's smoothness.

A rabbit burst from the woods. David looked where it had emerged and thought he saw a move- ment. Was it a deer? No, it was as large as a deer, but—he strained to see into the shadows under the trees—something taller. A bear? That would be a sighting!

But then the something moved, and a man stepped out from the shadows. A man about his own height who was staring intently at him.

MEETING

David felt awkward. He stared back at the man but then dropped his eyes. Bending down, he pretended to study the pile of stones at his feet, keeping the man in his peripheral vision. The stranger was still staring at him, and now he was walking toward him.

Was he from the hotel staff? What did he want? David straightened and looked at the approaching figure. The man could be his own twin, or at least a

brother, with his brown hair, sloping jaw, and wide
shoulders. Even the way he walked was similar,
though more energetic and determined. Yet as he
neared, David saw that although his face was physi-
cally somewhat like his, it was very different in its
energy and warmth.

When he drew close, the man stopped, keeping
his eyes on David, not saying anything. Finally, he
stooped to pick up a flat stone. He evaluated it
carefully, then dropped it. He kept searching and
finally settled on three very flat ones. With two in
one hand, he grasped the other between thumb and
finger as David had done and bent down.

The man spun the first off his finger with a snap
of the wrist similar to David's, but with his entire
body forcefully engaged. This was followed immediately by a blur of motion with which he snapped
off the other two stones with pistonlike precision.
One by one the stones spanked the water so hard
they were launched high into the air, all three in the
same trajectory, like birds flying in line off the lake.

The stranger turned toward him with a gregarious grin, but David felt fear. What a discomforting day this was. He was still trying to deal with the incredible lake phenomenon resonating in his consciousness and the whiff of that fragrance. Now this man had come up to him like an elite ranger . . . or maybe more like a host at a welcoming reception, to gauge by his expression. He was humming some tune David had never heard before.

Finally David said, "Good morning. Beautiful day, isn't it?"

"Beautiful and full of wonders!" the man responded. He turned his head to look at two geese with seven tiny goslings waddling slowly across the sandy shore. They all stepped into the water and then swam forward with one parent in front and the other behind.

"Do you live around here?" David asked.

The man smiled broadly. "Never been anywhere near here before." He slowly looked around, surveying the sky, the lake, and the forest, and then the birds and a rabbit nibbling grass nearby. "It's a place of beauty!"

Had he never been to a lake before? "Where are you from?" David asked.

The man laughed a hearty, infectious laugh. "A very different place," he declared. "It, too, has many wonders. You would love it."

A Baltimore oriole alighted on a nearby branch, its bright orange markings standing in contrast to its black feathers. David noticed the man watching the bird as it flew to another branch and then disappeared at the top of the tree.

"They're rare," David said. "We don't see them often here."

The man nodded. "Yes. Striking." The man's face and body seemed as if he were listening to music of some sort, his eyes merry, his head, hands, and feet slightly moving in rhythm.

Cottonwood seeds floated down around them like feathery snow. The man held out his hand and let some settle on it, then whirled around in the white tufts like an athlete spinning in triumph on the field. It reminded David of a day during his freshman year in college. His roommate, Werner, had come from

Brazil and had never seen snow. He eagerly antici-
pated it all through September and October, and
when the November day came that snow fell in thick
flakes, whitening the sky, Werner had run out of the
dorm and danced all around the building, arms flung
wide, shouting, "Snow! Snow! Snow!" David half
expected this man to start running the same way.

A squirrel began raucously scolding them from
high in a nearby oak. David looked up at it and gri-
maced at the annoyance.

The man also looked up, but with a great grin.
"That little fellow has a lot to tell us," he said.
"Urgent messages." Then he laughed again, his
laughter like a child's, capturing his whole body
so that it shook with merriment.

A phrase invaded David's mind: *brother squirrel*.
The stranger's laughter and good spirits made him
think of St. Francis of Assisi referring to all the
animals as brothers and sisters, as well as the sun
and moon and all creation. Like Francis, this guy
seemed to be coming from another century—or
was it a different planet?

Then another word centered itself in his mind: *holiness*.

Where'd that come from? *Holiness*? Why that word? Holiness brought to David's mind everything restrictive and austere, all the negatives of religious rigor and glumness. He supposed the thought of Francis had triggered the word. Was Francis holy? He guessed so, whatever that meant, though he certainly didn't think of St. Francis as glum.

Despite the man's warmth and smiles and delight in nature, David felt disoriented and uncomfortable. This stranger was looking into his eyes, studying as if probing not only his face but his inner thoughts and even his soul.

A sudden ripple of discord flashed across the man's face. It disappeared, replaced by a questioning look.

"Something wrong?" David asked.

The man said nothing.

David pressed him. "Why are you here? Do you work here?"

The man smiled and looked away toward two

rabbits frolicking across the grass. "Yes, I have been given work to do," he said. "Maybe for you."

What did he mean by that?

The man looked back at David's face, intensity in his eyes but a smile playing at the edges of his mouth. After a long silence, he nodded, turned, and strode briskly back into the woods.

FEAR

The waitress in the lodge's restaurant stood by his table, pad in hand. David said, "I'll have your veggie omelet, please. Moist, not dry."

"Our chef makes perfect omelets," she said with supreme confidence and a swirl of her pen. "And coffee?"

"Early and often."

She poured it and left. Having eaten the sweet

roll earlier that morning, he wasn't really ready
for an omelet, but he needed something. He
took a sip of coffee, noticed the trembling in his
hands, and set down the cup. This was supposed
to be decompression time? Instead of getting
refreshed, he was full of anxiety. He felt confused,
like a lab animal dropped into a strange environ-
ment. How was he to think about all the phenom-
ena outside?

In some ways, the man from the woods was
like a child. In fact, he seemed more innocent
and irrepressible than any child David had ever
come across. Yet he also sensed in the man
depths and capacities far beyond his own. The
way he had sent those stones into the air had been
disturbing.

After nibbling at the omelet, then pushing it
aside, David left the restaurant and stepped into the
gift shop. Flipping through magazines, he evaluated
the ads and editorials with a professional's eye rather
than that of a consumer. Yet, he smiled to himself,
he was also a consumer of magazines, the ads and

articles appealing to his needs and hungers. Food. Drink. Alluring women. Photos and words luring him to satisfy his desires.

In a similar way, he realized that something elemental in him longed for whatever was outside. He wanted to clear up the disorientation, to draw something good into the dark vacuum within. At the same time, he feared this stranger.

Out of the corner of his eye he saw fat Ed and his disagreeable companion Pete entering the restaurant. He was tempted to make a sarcastic comment as he walked past them, but they moseyed directly to a seat far in the back, and David slipped outside.

He wished he were talking right now with Marcia about all this. She would listen and at least be a sounding board, whereas no one here was likely to listen or care.

Outside, he peered around, thinking he would try to find the man, since he couldn't keep his mind off him. He would tramp the woods, and maybe the stranger would show up. After all, he'd said he had work to do for David—whatever that meant.

Actually, if the man was gone forever, maybe David could just heave a big sigh of relief.

Partway to the lake, he saw he wouldn't have to search. The man was sitting on a bench, looking toward the water. David moved toward him, churning inside over what would come of this, what he should say, and whether or not he should flee this place and drive straight back to Marcia.

The man looked up as David approached, then moved over to give him room. With a wry smile, he lifted his wrist toward David, turning it to reveal a thin ribbon of blood oozing from a red bite mark. "I grabbed a red squirrel by the tail," he explained. "He didn't like it."

David shook his head in sympathy. "Hurt much?"

The man didn't answer. Although he seemed buoyant and energetic as before, his expression was puzzled and strangely different. "Fear is there," he said soberly. "Fear in the forest."

"Oh?" David studied his face, trying to read it.

"I watched a hawk chase a blackbird into a bush. The little bird hid in thick branches, but the hawk kept flying into the bush. Finally it had the blackbird in its talons, quivering."

"Must have been quite a sight to witness that drama."

"The hawk killed it and flew off with it in its claws." The man pursed his lips, squinted against the sun, and sat silent. Finally he said, "The little bird was terrified."

David looked out at the gulls flying over the lake. "That's how the hawk has to eat. Fact is, we all eat something that first must die."

The man studied David's face and then looked down at the little droplets of blood on his wrist. "To die is to simply slip through a membrane into another world. Why the fear?"

What had the man said? "Slip through a membrane?" David had no idea how to answer his question. Who didn't fear death? What person, what creature, what microorganism for that matter, didn't flee from predators? And what did he mean, slipping though a membrane? On a sudden impulse he asked, "Did you just slip through a membrane?"

The man nodded, his eyes sparkling. "Not long before I saw you from the woods. Actually, it was more momentous than just slipping in!"

David squeezed his eyes shut for a moment, marveling at the man's words and reliving those spectacular moments of only a few hours before. He described to the man how startling the sounds, scents, and colors had been to him.

"Oh, you saw and heard? Some of my world came leaking in with me. But only for an instant. It wouldn't do to have it flowing in here." He paused, his fingers moving as if to some music from somewhere. "But you haven't answered my question. If death is just slipping through to another world, why all this fear?"

DISINTEGRATION

The man was full of questions David could not
answer. They came in nimble leaps, caroming off
one topic to probe a seemingly unrelated one. He
would leapfrog to yet another implication, obviously
a man with lots of analytical practice. David realized
that although the man knew little about the world he
had just entered, in many ways he knew far more
than David did.

"If the microbes on this planet are so uncon-
trolled and the science so elementary, what
plans—?"

"Every politician has plans and proposals,"
David interrupted. "Every science professor has
a project for Washington to fund."

"So how does the guidance flow—?"

David didn't let him finish this sentence either.
He felt as if he were handling a rapid-fire press
conference with no preparation and said, "Look,
maybe you should answer some of your own questions. You're way ahead of me on most of them."

The man shrugged. He exuded enormous
energy and, unlike David, seemed to delight in the
lively repartee. "In many ways ahead of you, yes.
In other ways, no."

David took a deep breath. "So why have you
come here?"

The man's smile carried a multitude of messages: a spirit of rising to a magnificent challenge, an
invitation for David to join him, a total confidence in
his own capacities. "Fear," he said. "Maybe the fear

is why I was sent. It is not just in the woods and the lake. I see it in your eyes."

David instantly dropped his gaze and happily spied a ladybug inching its way along the arm of the bench. He kept his eyes on it, putting his hand down and blocking its way so that it had to crawl onto his finger. For a moment he watched the insect starting to crawl through the hairs on the back of his hand. Then he asked the man, "Don't you ever feel fear?"

"No," the stranger said gently, but he didn't elaborate. Instead he put his finger beside the ladybug, lifted it, and slowly launched it into the air. "Someday, perhaps, you also will not know fear."

David studied the complexities of the remarkable man's face, so similar to his own yet so unique. Who, or what, was this man? "Who are you—really—and where have you come from?" he asked.

"Worlds unknown here, I suspect." The man cocked his head as if a little mystified himself.

His response sent David's imagination roaming over the many fantasy films and books he'd

absorbed through the years. Then there were the
stories of angels. Might he be an angel? Might that
explain all this?

Fantasy stuff, he thought. *All those books on
angels, all those stories of strangers rescuing people
and children having visions of heavenly beings. Never
objective journalism—just tales. People simply name
Good Samaritans angels.*

As a lit major he had read plenty of supernatural
stories, including a few Stephen King books. He
knew a fair amount about religious history and had
always been skeptical of angel stories, including
those in the ancient literature.

Yet what might explain this strange, strange
man? He wondered if any of the old tales came anywhere near the reality of what he was hearing. Or
was it reality? In fact, was this person even real, or
was he having the ultimate hallucination out on this
bench in front of that very real lodge behind him?
David noticed his hand was shaking a little as he
asked, "So what is your name?"

The man pursed his lips with a smile, as if taking

up a challenge. "What would you like it to be? Give me a name—a good one," he invited, "one you think fits me well."

David hadn't expected that. What would fit this man? What person from history or a movie or a novel was he most like? Actually, no one, he concluded, yet he liked the idea of giving him a name. In his mind he rambled through multiple names and finally, looking into the man's eyes to check his response, he said, "You're Michael."

The man's eyes crinkled agreeably. "Okay. Why?"

"Because Michael's an angel. Actually, an archangel, whatever that is." David paused, still watching his eyes. "Are you an angel?"

The man David had named Michael smiled. "Maybe." He turned his palms up and out in a gesture. "I'm told that's what they call celestials here."

At that, David's whole body tingled in both alarm and hope. He slowly, slowly digested the implications and finally said, "I thought angels knew everything."

"No one but the Maker knows everything."

Michael tilted his head as if in apology. "I'm not from this universe, so naturally I don't know what your angels know."

"But surely you've heard about this world."

Michael tipped his head back, and his eyes danced. "Have you any idea how vast the Creator's creations are? Trillions of stars glow in billions of galaxies—and that's just your universe! How many worlds? How many celestials? You yourself have trillions of tiny creatures within your own body." He laughed as he opened his hands and spread them apart. "Yet we have heard that some angels here know very deep mysteries. I imagine this archangel Michael you mentioned knows secrets that in our dimensions we haven't even guessed at!"

David was taken aback. What in the world was he talking about? "You say strange things if you're an angel."

Michael smiled. "Maybe I'm not an angel. Maybe I'm just one more of the Creator's celestial worshipers. There are all sorts of us," he said with a lively flourish of his hand and added agreeably, "Call me what you will!"

Angels. Saints. Sinners. Religious beliefs. What was happening here? David had always prided himself on being rational about such things. The closest he had ever come to a religious experience was resonating with the profound ecstasy of Father Zosima in *The Brothers Karamazov.* He viewed religion and the paranormal as fascinating subjects for *National Geographic.* They were mysteries to be analyzed and carefully put into context by the PhDs who packaged comprehensive overviews for the Smithsonian.

But angels? Angels and demons were simply cultural myths, weren't they? Only superstitious people believed in angels.

David watched his mysterious companion looking with fascination at blackbirds filling a nearby tree and said to him, "You're frustrating me. Maybe you're faking that you don't know about pain and evil. We've all heard about bad angels—demons— the ones that try to seduce us."

This accusation made Michael's face a study in innocent perplexity. "Bad angels?" he asked.

In a rush of words David said, "Maybe you're not a good angel at all. Maybe you're a demon, and maybe the Maker you talk about is actually a Darth Vader. I don't know. Maybe if I were smart, I'd run back to my room!"

Michael stared at him with a quizzical expression. "But what do you mean by *good* and *bad*?"

This was maddening. Nonsensical. Threatening. How could this man speak perfectly good English with multiple nuances of meaning, demonstrating sophisticated brilliance, yet not know the concepts of good and evil? This surreal juncture made David feel it was he who had entered a different world.

David's words exploded. "How in the world can you be an angel if you don't know the difference between good and bad?"

Michael was unruffled, looking at David as if fascinated by his emotions. "The Father has chosen to reveal to me vast knowledge—but only in my own dimensions. He created me as one who helps His created souls to develop new, dynamic worlds." He raised his chin in satisfaction. "That's what I've been doing. And now I've been sent on this pioneer mission here."

David tried to visualize what he was talking about. He kept focused on the man's face, trying to decipher clues to what really went on behind those eyes. "So how can you not know—?"

"We did once hear something about rebellious angels, but that never concerned us. We've been creating in our Creator's powers, singing His glories, listening for His signals, fulfilling His grand purposes." He sat poised like an athlete, his body language saying he was ready for anything. "The greatest wonder of all," he said, "more than all the challenge, music, and creativity, is being in harmony with the One who loves us."

David squared his shoulders and set his jaw, as if he needed to rise to match at least a little of the man's energy, whose smile included a slightly sheepish look as he said, "I admit I've wondered about your mysterious world, so different from all of ours. We all desire to find out what's been going on here." He reached out to touch David's shoulder. "So I'm here to learn . . . and to help."

David felt so many surging emotions he didn't know what his mind was telling him. He resonated with this man's spirit, yet he felt uneasy and on guard.

Michael asked David where he ate and slept, and soon they were walking toward the lodge, then through the sliding glass door into his room.

The celestial picked up the telephone and inspected it, then the TV remote. David took it from his hand, plugged in the TV, and pushed the power button. As the screen came alive, David wondered if Michael knew anything about technology. He showed him how to switch channels, and Michael immediately took the remote from his hand.

The man soon was watching a BBC world news report and was riveted for nearly a half hour by stories of an attempted assassination, a kidnapping, two religious riots, accusations of bribery, villagers raped and killed, and refugees attacked by soldiers. After watching all that without comment, Michael turned toward David with a grieved look. "Has this ever happened before?" he asked.

"Every day," David said flatly.

Michael kept channel surfing while David sat on the bed, the screen skipping intermittently from talk shows to drama to history to commentary. Finally David interrupted during a commercial, which the man was watching as analytically as the programming. "What do you think of all this?"

Michael's eyes turned toward David, their ebullient twinkle and merriment gone. He did not respond to the question but remained silent and still except for an enigmatic movement of his brows. Pressing the remote's power button, he watched the screen blink to gray and said slowly, "I've a great deal to learn about good and bad. . . ." This last phrase lingered unfinished.

David had been wondering how advanced this man was, and he began to get an answer after he had given him the computer password, showed him the basics, and then located an online encyclopedia. Michael held the key down and rushed through it in a blur, then read through a dictionary the same way. As he got a feel for the computer, he started calling up documents and connections.

"You use computers in your world?"

The stranger pursed his lips as his fingers manipulated the keyboard. "Our communication devices are quicker and more powerful." He smiled as he scrolled the screens, adding enigmatically, "But they're self-powered."

David sat down again, this time in the chair by the window, feeling once again as if he were in some kind of movie he couldn't understand. Michael kept scanning data, scrolling quickly through literature, history, art, and science. David was amazed at his dexterity, scanning the material as quickly as it appeared so that, to David, the computer screen was a blur of words and images.

This went on and on, and David tired of watching. "Are you finding what you're looking for?" he asked.

"I don't know what I'm looking for. But I am stunned by what I'm finding."

Michael resumed his rapid research, but then added without looking at David, "Clearly, the enigmas of fear and good and evil are astounding, and their meaning unclear, despite all this endless analysis."

"You should read *War and Peace*."

"Already have," he said as he continued reading online in a blur of screens.

David found that astonishing. He noticed the Bible on the table not far from the computer and pointed to it. "That's where many get their beliefs about good and evil."

"Yes, I know," he said. "There are countless references to it, and I will study it closely." He picked it up and scanned the pages as he had the Web sites, but then closed it and tucked it under his arm. "I need some fresh air," he said, moving toward the door. "But I'll find you again today. I am here because of you, you know." And with that he was gone.

REVELATION

David thought about movies he had watched. There he would be, a huge theater screen in front of him, immersed in a Russian landscape with thousands of Cossacks attacking, or in an exotic jungle, or on some strange planet with bizarre creatures inspecting the humans. Now he was immersed in an ordinary room, but he felt he had been transported into a movie, and he was wishing the final credits would start rolling so this would all be over and he could walk away.

At the same time, David was intrigued and drawn to this remarkable stranger. Maybe he should just get into his car and escape to Marcia and share all this with her. Yet hearing his story, she might be tempted to call for the guys in the white coats.

He stepped into the sunlight, not knowing what to do or think, and circled the lodge to the trailhead of the longest loop through the forest. As he walked, he still worried that Michael might not be as benign as he appeared. He seemed to be good, but this story about his being an angel from other worlds was bizarre. And didn't seductive demons tell you stories as they led you to, and over, a cliff? Was he being tempted somehow? Was this guy a hallucination? After all, people having hallucinations found them very, very real.

He wished Michael would just give him some sort of angelic blessing, maybe tell him what he was supposed to do and then let him get on with his life. Yet seeing him watch the news with its horrors and tragedies made David think the man really was an innocent seeing this tormented world for the first time.

He ended up sitting on the bench by the lake again. Swallows were skimming the water, snatching bugs out of the air. Two were chasing each other, darting and frolicking with remarkably sharp and swift turns and dives. *At least they seem happy*, he thought.

One of the swallows swooped down on a speck of white on the water. David saw that it was a tiny curled feather from one of the ducks. The bird scooped up the feather and rose high above the water, but then David saw the feather floating down. "He realized it wasn't a little meal after all," he said aloud. But then the swallow arced back, snatched the feather in the air, and sped off, the other swallow in hot pursuit. He was just playing with the feather, David thought. Strange how this world could be so full of beauty and frolic and love yet terribly intermixed with all the horror on TV.

When he finally trudged back to his room, he

saw through the window that Michael was inside, the Bible in his hand. David watched him. Unlike all the scanning Michael had done, this time he was staring at one open page.

David unlocked the door, and as he entered, the man looked up. His face was powerfully altered yet inscrutable.

"How did you get in?" David asked. "The door was locked."

"Maybe I walked through the wall."

Did David detect sardonic humor? Or could Michael, who moved so easily from one universe to another, actually walk through a wall? He supposed angels could.

"You've read the Bible?" David asked.

"Many times."

David visualized his quickly flipping through those hundreds of pages. "What are you looking at?" he asked, pointing to the open Bible.

Elbow on the desk, Michael pressed his chin against his knuckles and stared at David. "Jesus wept," he said.

There was a long, long silence. David tried to plumb what was behind Michael's expression. What was it? Awe? Wonder? Distress?

"It's in your Bible," Michael said.

David nodded.

"Jesus wept," he said again.

Whatever profound meaning those words had for Michael was escaping David. He saw on the visitor's face intense expressions worthy of a Rembrandt masterpiece, but . . .

Michael lowered his eyes, then raised his head and looked out the window. David followed his gaze and saw two dogs chasing each other down the path to the lake.

"Jesus had so much to weep about," Michael said.

The dogs were now splashing in the water. One came out and shook itself.

Michael said with a strange tightness in his face and shoulders, "After His weeping and all the love that Jesus kept giving to all these wounded ones, your people murdered Him."

A stab of fear sliced into David's midsection. The stranger's statement was flat, not accusatory in tone, but the stark weight of it struck him like a blow.

"Do you realize," Michael asked, "that this is the Beloved? Our Beloved? And the Beloved, as your Bible says, of the Father above?"

Michael slowly laid the Bible beside the computer. "You know the whole story. The shame and humiliation. The Beloved subjecting Himself to the whip and the nails, to the agony and ignominy. . . ." Michael's facile mind for once seemed unable to express itself. The seismic shadings of such an unthinkable paradox darkened his face. "That He would come as a baby, that He would endure this world and go to His death at such brutal hands! None of His creatures in any dimension could have imagined it."

David was astounded at the awe permeating the man, at the way the familiar story had affected someone so advanced beyond his own capacities. David sat down on the bed, and for long moments, neither said anything.

Finally Michael said, "This corrupted world! Why didn't the Beloved destroy it, make this world a cinder in the winds?" He sat back in his chair. "It's a mystery far beyond me."

David looked out the window at a V of geese flying high above the lake.

"Amazing grace," Michael continued. "You sing of it, but the Beloved's humiliation transformed into His glory . . . It's far beyond amazing."

David nodded, not knowing quite what he was nodding about; then Michael added, "But, of course, you know all that."

David supposed he did know all that, but not like this.

"Your Bible says Jesus did it 'because of the joy awaiting Him,'" Michael said. "Is that right?"

David had no idea how to answer. He had said "your Bible"? But it wasn't his Bible; it was the lodge's Bible. And although David knew something about its content, he realized this man now knew far more than he did. He struggled with his desire to flee the room. Instead of answering David asked,

"How do you know all this is true? Many of the most learned among us think Jesus was just a very good man who was tragically executed."

Michael immediately shot back, "Is that what you think?"

David sighed, reeling from so many unexpected sallies. "I've never known what to think. It all happened two thousand years ago!"

"But," Michael said, "it's all still happening— right now."

THE CALL

Now Michael was the one answering questions, describing how the drama of the Creator's work on planet earth intersected with so many other unique worlds.

David's mind whirled. Slowly he felt his spirit energized, as if he were in the eye of a benevolent hurricane lifting him into purpose and energy. At the same time David felt overwhelmed and agitated, wanting to flee to a warm, dark place, to go back to his sleep under the covers.

Michael told him that reading about Jesus in the Scriptures had amazed him but also had given him a dramatically new paradigm for his Maker's love.

As Michael spoke of the dynamism between the Son and the Father, David sensed the celestial was once again resonating with music.

Lifting his chin, Michael said, "Praising Father, Son, and Spirit is the music of all worlds."

"You sound like a theologian," David said.

"I've studied your New Testament, and it resonates with reality. And I've read your theologians trying to grasp the mysteries of the Trinity. They struggle toward what cannot be grasped, but they are right to keep struggling." He said this with a crinkling in his eyes and the same infectious sense of wonder as when he had whirled among the cottonwoods.

The man talked like a pastor or a priest, and David wasn't sure he liked where this might be going. He looked out the window at the swallows darting through the air to catch their little snacks, putting an end to countless insect lives. An old quote came to his mind, and he said, "Einstein put the ultimate question this way: 'Is the universe friendly?' You're telling me it's more than friendly— that everything emanates from extravagant love." He picked up the Bible Michael had been holding and waved it back and forth. "Where is it? Where is this extravagant love for His world? You've seen what's on TV?"

Michael responded instantly, "This creation still groans!" He took the Bible from David's hand and flipped its pages. "Your world awaits its redemption."

To David, all this sounded familiar, the words of Christmas and Easter, of cathedrals and chapels, yet they astounded him, coming from this man from another world. He felt amazed and intrigued, yet disoriented, torn in two directions. On the one hand, how could he possibly question an angel, if that's what Michael was? On the other, this wasn't some angel helping a victim at an accident. David felt he was being invaded.

"You, too, are a son of the Father," Michael was saying. He paused a moment, then added, "But I am simply telling you what is in your own Scriptures."

David nodded. "Yes, and Dostoyevsky and St. Francis and smart believers all through the centuries have resonated with it. But look at how screwy even Tolstoy became over religion. Where has it left this sorry world? Why does it so often fuel hatred and stupidity?"

Michael looked so intensely into David's eyes that he felt penetrated. Michael said without accusation but with very personal intent, "Each and every soul here must be reconciled to the Father."

David felt relieved when this forceful creature finally relaxed his gaze, eased back, and then smiled. "Let's take a walk. I'd like to see everything here."

As they walked along a pathway leading to some shops near the lodge, David prompted, "Tell me about where you come from."

"I was present when the Creator made my world. I was there as the first two became living souls."

"Adam and Eve?"

With a start Michael said, "No, no, no! I've read Genesis. Your ancestors fell from the Creator's love. Evil distorts everything here. No, in my world the two were obedient. They started as two and I was there to help them overcome staggering challenges. Now they fill untold planets, and they've traveled into other dimensions."

"Slipping through membranes?" David said wryly.

Michael cocked his head in assent. "And I have always gone with them."

"So what's it like—in worlds beyond this one?"

They had walked into a music store, and Michael picked up a flute. "Music. Vitality—great vitality. You've heard descriptions of heaven, but they're broad brushstrokes. There are too many worlds to even begin to describe their originality. One of your writers used the phrase 'mind-boggling immensities' for your astronomers' discoveries. They'd find those in universe after universe—immensities and complexities!"

David had read articles himself. "Those observers say our universe is not only expanding," he said, "but expanding faster and faster, and that what we can observe—our universe—may be just a glimmer of something much, much greater."

"Exactly!" Michael said, as if savoring marvelous news. "And all just a thin veil away." He put down the flute and looked at David with commiseration. "But your world is unique. You don't just slip through a membrane. Death is the enemy here, the ultimate curse from the rebellion. It's all in your Scriptures." The celestial put his hand on David's shoulder. "Yours is the land of the dying. Here, the Father's originality is everywhere, yet death stalks the forest, and death stalks your homes and cities."

David couldn't conceptualize the alternative. "But without death," he asked, "how can a world renew itself? Without fear, without competition, without force and counterforce, how—?"

Michael nodded vigorously, interrupting. "No one on earth has experienced a world without these things. Here, you live in distortion. But on God's other worlds, challenges abound. David, you couldn't conceive of a tiny part of those universe-size challenges." He stopped suddenly and with an expansive smile brought his hands together in a sharp clap. "And the challenges are met. They are overcome in the magnificent powers of the Creator. In the harmony of the Father of lights, from whom all good things and all energies flow, all is possible!"

To David, that was dumbfounding. "All?" he asked.

Michael was flipping through some Bach cantata scores. "This is wonderful," he said. "But it is just a taste of the wonders. In my worlds, there is no end to music, to expanding dimensions."

"But here in our world," David objected, "and in the vast reaches of the stars and galaxies we can observe, we—"

"You are lost. Here in your universe is a great emptiness. Evil powers rule. All the promise of your first two was corrupted. But now the magnificent rescue! I cannot absorb even a portion of the wonder of what the Father sent Jesus to do."

They left the music shop and walked to a stand selling fruit. David bought them each an apple and crunched down on his. "You've been sent here to tell us all this?"

"To tell *you*, David. You are the one listening to me. God's creatures are numberless, all quick to do the Father's bidding. This archangel Michael—I see that your Bible reveals him as one of the great ones. I've never met him, yet all of us move in the same harmony."

As they entered a bookstore, David let his mind play with scenarios of numberless persons in countless worlds without evil. He just couldn't grasp it. "Are all your peoples unaware of tragedy and pain?"

Michael put his hand firmly on David's shoulder. "I don't know why we've been so blessed! I'd heard little more than a whisper of the rebellion in this world."

David digested that statement and finally said, "You're blessed indeed!"

Michael headed for the art section, where he looked with appreciation at oversize volumes of

Monet, van Gogh, Turner, Sargent, and Michelangelo. He grinned as he paged through a thick retrospective of Norman Rockwell and then flipped through a stack of scenic photography books.

After scanning volumes on religion and philosophy, Michael moved to the Bible section. "In your Scriptures, Paul says the creation here groans as in childbirth, but in the cascade of universes, there is no groaning, only music." Michael spoke with brisk energy. "From sphere to sphere we praise and build, all things unique to each culture. All dimensions are filled with the Maker's glory. So we are to be holy, as the Beloved is holy."

For David, all this cathedral talk in a bookstore amazed and tantalized him, filled him with hope but also threatened him.

"What do you mean by *holy*?" he asked.

"Having unity with the One. Holiness is what you long for. To be free of the rebellion's decay, to see through the eyes of God, and to be delighted in His life coursing through you."

David absorbed that slowly. He surely did have

longings, but also discomfort, as if he were being dragged before a judge.

Michael started leafing through finance, food, and general-interest magazines. When he picked up a gaudy soft-porn publication, David felt embarrassed as he watched him flip the pages.

Michael replaced it with an odd grimace. "Beautiful women," he said. "Deadly celebration."

They walked on, and Michael stepped into a toy store. He smiled as noises of a cow, dog, sheep, and cat sounded when he pressed their shapes. Looking through children's books of animals and stories, he said, "No wonder Jesus declared, 'The Kingdom of God belongs to those who are like these children.'"

They left the toy store, then briskly walked through a clothing store and a photography shop. Michael finally indicated with a shrug of his shoulders he was ready to go. In a few moments they ended up once again on the bench by the lake.

"Michael, why me?" David asked, trying to come to grips with this extraordinary visitation. "Why were you sent to me?"

Michael flipped up his palms and gave a little infectious laugh. "You were the one who sensed my coming. You said it was loud and that colors splashed the sky, yet you were the only one who saw or heard." He paused. "Or wanted to see and hear. Perhaps you were ready. Perhaps you are called. Perhaps you are the only one here who has ears and eyes open."

David gave no response but quietly watched the geese on the lake.

"I suspect you are called to great things. You have always longed for that, and perhaps God has noticed." He gripped David's forearm. "Listen to the music," Michael said quietly. "Can you hear it?"

David remained silent. He didn't hear music, but he did hear a call. However, it was but one stream of the turbulence churning within.

Finally David said, "I'm listening."

"Listen well."

David took a very deep breath and then exhaled, as if relieving his chest of all the strange turbulence. "The call is chaotic. I hear it, but what can I do?

What can anyone really do these days? The whole world seems to be sliding into terrorist anarchy, the planet overloaded and hurtling toward meltdown. My hopes—all our hopes—keep getting crushed."

"Of course!" Michael said. "The enemy's power constantly corrupts everything here. He delights in crushing your hopes and luring you into his hopelessness." The celestial slowly lifted his hands and brought them tightly together. "You are being called to magnificent hope. Your hand can interlock with the Maker's. You can respond to His initiatives just as I do." He then stretched his arms wide apart and swept them across the expanse of the clouded sky. "All the despair—all the trillions upon trillions of bitter tears on this earth—all will be swallowed up. But before that, you have great things to do."

David hadn't admitted his fear of being controlled, of becoming chained by restrictions instead of remaining free to do "great things." He sat silently, staring at the lake and the clouds, wondering at the incongruity of his sitting beside this magnificent person from God yet being tormented by warring forces.

He looked over at the visitor. Michael's eyes were closed tight as he said to David very quietly, "I never could have grasped the fathomless depth of His love."

"What do you mean?"

"The creativity and advancements of my peoples would fill you with awe. Yet this world's drama and the terrible warfare here is beyond imagination! I've always moved and worshiped and rejoiced in the love of Father, Son, and Spirit. But to learn what the Beloved suffered here to bring joy . . ." Michael said nothing more. His thumbs were on his chin, his fingers making a tent beneath his eyes.

David watched him for a time, then asked, "Are you praying?"

Michael smiled. "Yes. I am always praying."

"What about?"

"Just now, my prayers are for you."

That's what I was afraid of, David thought. Yet it was also what he longed for.

"Your soul is struggling with the great powers," the celestial said sympathetically. He closed his eyes and placed the heel of his hand firmly against his own forehead. "How do I know this? Angels of the rebellion have now begun trying to lure me to join their side. But I've been warned. I've been praying and resisting." Michael dropped his hand and opened his eyes, looking intently at David. "That's why I've been praying."

David stared straight ahead, trying to process what Michael said. "Actually, I never would have thought angels prayed."

Michael smiled. "Of course angels pray. Jesus prayed. If the Son of God communes with His Father, if He prays for those His Father has given Him—as we know He does—then surely I can pray for you." He smiled again. "I have also learned that even here on this corrupted world, prayer brings clarity and the Spirit's power, and it summons cosmic allies who are here with us right now!"

David felt overwhelmed by all Michael was saying and the cacophony of messages in his mind.

They had been sitting for a long time, and suddenly he stood, trying to shake from his body all this strange and sobering talk, trying to get his emotions stabilized. "I'm hungry," he said. "Let's go get a sandwich."

Michael shook his head no and leaned back on the bench. "You go. But let me pray for you first." Michael looked straight ahead, eyes open but tight in concentration, and prayed aloud. "Loving Father above; Beloved Son beside; Holy Spirit within . . . reveal Your power and love to David."

With that simple prayer, he turned to David and said, "Go, and as you do, listen for the Father's voice. Listen for the call."

David hesitantly stepped away. He wished Michael were joining him, but at the same time he wanted a breather. He started up the path, feeling torn in many directions by all he had heard and experienced.

Before David had gone far, Michael added, "David, don't be afraid. You are chosen. Open yourself. Listen. Listen for the music."

NIGHT

Behind the deli counter, a bored teenage girl with a ponytail looked up as David entered. He smiled at her and said, "Looks like it's slow in here." She returned his smile, and David asked, "Could you make me a ham and cheese on wheat? Lots of veggies?"

The girl nodded and selected some ham while David surveyed the lettuce, carrots, sprouts, green

peppers, olives, and condiments. They looked
familiar, comforting, like the girl's smile. But the
inner turbulence kept churning—desire and dread,
longing and fear—and a claustrophobic compulsion
to break free. But free to what? Michael's energies
and hope had stormed into David's life like some
unstoppable yet benign force. He wanted to
embrace all the celestial's promises, to welcome into
his spirit and soul all that Michael had said was possible. Yet other voices whispered that he would lose
too much, whispered about what he'd have to give
up. The whispers intrigued him with an illicit tang
he didn't want to lose.

"Which veggies?" the girl asked.

He pointed one by one to what he wanted.
When the girl reached for the condiments, he said,
"Just honey mustard."

Maybe if I eat, he thought, *I'll be able to deal
with this better.*

The girl was wrapping the sandwich when
David heard footsteps. He turned to see the old
men, Pete and Ed, slowly making their way to a

small table nearby. They sat down heavily, and Ed picked up a newspaper.

Before David could turn and escape with his sandwich, Pete glanced over and saw him. The old man's body stiffened, like a mastiff suddenly aware of a rabbit. Keeping his eyes fixed on David, he turned his chair slightly while elbowing Ed.

David ground his teeth. His face reddened, intensifying his embarrassment. Neither man said a word as he walked past, but their smugness infuriated him. Even when he was past them and nearly out the door, he felt their brazen stares on his back, like stinging tentacles on his neck.

He strode quickly to a nearby table, unwrapped the sandwich, and bit at it savagely. The whispers within him became visceral. What was Michael really sucking him into? As he ate the sandwich, a flood of images from religion's excesses filled his mind, from the Inquisition and the Crusades to religious mobs of all creeds throughout history murdering innocent families. Did David want such extreme spirituality? He thought of all those crazies who stared into the sun or crawled in bloody agony to atone for sins, and all those calculating "holy" enforcers of their own versions of godliness.

The questioning whispers grew urgent. *Think about St. Francis. Forget his love of nature, and consider the saint's weirdness. Do you really want to strip off your clothes, renouncing all pleasures and possessions, and beg your way through life because of a strange angel visitation? Why waste your life? Forget ever going to Las Vegas for some fun! Francis, Mother Teresa, monks chanting in silence all day—are those what you want?*

This holiness Michael said he longed for—what would it require of him?

As a boy, David had lifted rocks in the grass to see what was underneath. Sometimes he would see a white worm suddenly removed from darkness and exposed to the glaring sun, writhing under its light. He felt like that worm.

This is ridiculous! David thought. All his life he'd wanted to make a strong contribution, and now with Michael nearby, all he could think of was his loss of freedom and how scary God's demands might be. The whispers grew more and more insistent, burning in his gut.

He finished the sandwich, took a napkin out of the bag, tossed the wrapper and bag into a trash canister, and stepped outside. At the lake, he saw Michael standing next to the bench, legs apart, arms spread upward. David knew he should start his legs moving toward him. How could he not? Yet he kept hesitating.

Not yet, he thought. *Not just yet.*

He wiped the corners of his mouth with the napkin, keeping his eyes on Michael's muscular form. David had always longed to make his mark, to rise to a great challenge, to be a hero on a stallion like Washington or Lee leading anxious troops, doing things his own way. But the whispers said he'd never do anything his own way if he walked down that path to Michael.

Wretched whispers! Were they demonic? He didn't know, but he was amazed at their power. He felt defiled, torn between two compelling desires.

He didn't want to connect with Michael feeling this way. He wanted to run somewhere, to think everything through and deal with all this craziness on his own terms. Staring at Michael, he knew he should go down there, and he did long for holiness . . . maybe.

But not quite yet.

Suddenly he turned on his heel and walked briskly toward the woods. He would take the trail down the hill. What could it hurt? He would come back soon. He wanted new stimuli and fresh air pumping in his lungs; he wanted to run from everything that had happened.

Run he did, dodging rocks and branches on the trail, feeling the rush of air in his face.

He stopped when he saw resting against a tree a length of stick the thickness of his wrist. *Walking stick,* he thought, but as he picked it up, he remembered another use for a stick like this. As a boy he had used one to whack dead branches and saplings.

He grasped the stick, plunged off the trail, and attacked a long-dead sapling caught in the

branches of a live oak. *Whack!* He split it in two,
the top half flipping against the oak. *Whack!*
Whack! Whack! He ran at dead branches and
small trees, splitting them into pieces, finding more
and more of them and hitting with all his might for
so long that his hands grew sweaty and slippery.
He imagined two fat old men falling ludicrously
into the dirt. Finally he gave a tremendous whack
at a big dead tree he knew wouldn't break, but he
took great satisfaction at the way its bark splintered
in a cloud of dust.

Brandishing his trusty stick, he looked around
in satisfaction at the broken pieces of wood and
searched for the trail. Soon he was following it
steeply downhill beneath bur oaks. After descend-
ing for a time, he estimated he should be getting
close to the road and stopped to listen for the
sound of cars and trucks at the big service-station
complex. Ahead, the trail curved back the other
way and uphill, starting another loop.

He peered through the foliage to see if the road
was nearby but saw nothing but woods. A trail

bench was positioned under a nearby maple, so he
eased himself down onto it.

Well, he thought, *I'm not with Michael, but here
I am on a bench.*

A squirrel rustled some oak leaves. A robin
landed on the trail and pecked at something. Near
his feet, a cluster of pink lady slippers moved with
the breeze at the base of the maple. "Lady slippers—the perfect name," he whispered aloud. The
wildflowers were indeed shaped like a slipper, with
ridges like stitching. Whenever he saw lady slippers,
he would envision one of those tiny English fairies
slipping a delicate pink slipper onto her foot, the
white top flaring around the fairy's ankle.

"Listen," Michael had said. "Listen for the
music."

David was listening, but he heard no music.
He heard only squirrels and birds and inner voices
warring within.

One of them was Michael's. He'd told David
that Jesus warned against people with eyes that
cannot see and ears that cannot hear, but He had

blessed those with ears that hear and eyes that see. What did that mean? Wasn't David the one who had seen Michael slip into this world? Wasn't he the one who had heard sounds no one else had?

Faint hums in the distance caught his attention. Was that the sound of tires on a road? Maybe he'd go down to the service station and get a Coke. It wouldn't take long.

He spied a deer trail and figured it was going toward the road. Sure enough, after about five minutes of ducking under branches and clambering over rocks, he spotted a passing car through the foliage. A few more minutes, and he emerged on the road.

The service station was past a wide curve, up on a hill. He walked there, lingered in the store while drinking his Coke, then came back to the place he thought he had emerged from the woods. Slowly walking along the forest edge, he kept peering into the woods to find the deer trail. However, all he saw were bushes and leaves. The growth was thick all along the road.

David looked back at the service station, trying

to judge where he had come out. It was getting dark, and finally in frustration he decided he would bush-whack his way through the relatively short distance to the main trail. He leaned forward, crashed through some burdock and elderberry bushes, then found places for his feet as he bent and twisted his way through the dense foliage. Pushing aside branches and climbing around rock formations, he searched for the deer trail but couldn't find it.

David kept moving, but after another ten min-utes in the darkening forest, he realized he had not only missed the deer trail but had somehow missed the main trail as well.

He stopped and looked in all directions. Noth-ing indicated one direction was better than another.

A little edge of panic appeared. The sun was almost gone; he couldn't tell east from west. Only by looking up through the trees could he see light, and the sky was darkening.

He tried to visualize how the trails were laid out. They extended for miles, and he didn't know how they all connected. He had heard horror stories of people getting lost in forests like this. After all, it was a state park with thousands of acres, and he had read over and over to never go off the trails.

And he hadn't really left the trail. He had simply tried to bushwhack a short way to one. But now he had no idea which direction to go.

A steep hill to his left seemed as good an option as any. He climbed it, stumbling in the near dark and pushing through brambles and low branches. It was sweaty work. He kept trudging uphill through the crackling leaves, and finally the ground under him leveled out. He looked around. Still no indication of a trail, nothing that might orient him.

A new thought expanded the edge of panic. If he had been bearing the wrong way, he might already have missed the trails and be partway into the mountains that went on for miles. Maybe he should just stop moving.

He sat down on a dead tree that was sunk into the leafy debris. He no longer knew what was left or right, let alone east or west.

For long moments he sat, concentrating on how

to get out of this fix. It was almost completely dark. He wondered if he should just stay right here and wait till morning, an uncomfortable option but better than getting far into the mountains and taking forever to find civilization.

Civilization. The more he learned of it, the more he grasped existential despair. The senselessness of people's suffering had always eaten at him, intensified over the past few years by the daily news of wrenching calamities. His knowledge of history only aggravated his despair as images played in his mind: young men marching off to endure warfare and torture; women racked by grief; children born into sure starvation; untouchables in India living in unspeakable shame; Stalin, Mao, Hitler, Hussein—an endless list of tyrants.

He laughed dryly and said aloud, "'Hope springs eternal'—a memorable phrase only because it's so outrageous. Yes, this is the land of the dying—and the desperate."

He dug his fingernails into the bark of the log, feeling he couldn't sit any longer. He decided he'd have to take a chance on direction and started walking again, but now it was so dark he couldn't see anything overhead. It had been threatening rain, and although the forecast hadn't predicted it, clouds now obscured the heavens.

He moved cautiously in the darkness, straining his eyes up to catch a faint light at the tops of the trees.

Lost!

He was angry at himself. How could he be so stupid as to get lost? A root snared his foot, tipping him forward so that he almost sprawled on the ground. He groaned and shoved aside a thick branch.

Every time his foot hit a root or a fallen branch embedded in the debris, he thought of snakes surrounding him. He didn't like snakes. And what else might be in this forest, in this darkness? What other hungry thing might be coming up from the undergrowth? No, he would not stop; he would keep moving.

Yet he felt he was getting nowhere, that he would

be moving all night, his feet constantly hitting obstructions and his hands groping against clinging vines and spiderwebs and bushes with thin, prickly whips.

He stopped, drew his sleeve across his forehead to wipe off the sweat.

Fear.

Yes, Michael was right. Birds, chipmunks—they all knew they were hunted in the night. He felt like one of them, alone and unprotected in the dark. His body was lost. His soul was lost.

Michael had said to listen. He had said not to be afraid. But David *was* afraid. He was alone in the dark forest. He had gotten himself here, far from the trail and from Michael's message of love and grace.

David remembered Michael's talking about Jesus' parable of Lazarus and the rich man—how Abraham had told the rich man that if his brothers wouldn't believe the Scriptures and the prophets, they wouldn't believe even if someone rose from the dead! With horror, David realized he was like them. He had been told all these wondrous things.

A celestial being, full of power and joy, had told him of ultimate reconciliation in this tortured world, reminded him of all those Christmas peace-on-earth pronouncements that sounded so warm and wonderful in the season but disappeared in the New Year revelries. Here David had heard the message that would bring him peace, and he had walked away from it.

"Father!" David suddenly called out aloud. "Father!"

As Michael had prayed to the Father, and as Jesus had prayed to the Father, so David called out to Him. He stood in the darkness saying how empty and senseless and painful his life was, how desperate he was not only for the Father to find him in the night forest but to be found as Michael was found, full of meaning and joy and music.

Music. Listen.

David listened, but he heard no music.

At the same time, the murmuring voices were gone, and he felt a release in his chest. He groped in the darkness for what he thought was a fallen tree, found it, and sat down unsteadily. His hands shook. He prayed as Michael had prayed:

> *"Loving Father above;*
> *Beloved Son beside;*
> *Holy Spirit within . . ."*

He paused. Then he said into the darkness, "Come. Come into my soul."

David sat praying for a long time, tears wetting his face as he admitted his stubborn will and his self-absorption. While he prayed, he began to feel aspirations and desires, astringent and sweet, rising like a tiny bit of white steam from fresh coffee.

He started at the rustle of wings not far away. An owl, perhaps? Slowly, he walked in that direction.

He went over in his mind all that Michael had told him. *So much to remember,* he thought. *So much to absorb.* He prayed that he would have at least a portion of the joy and power and connection his remarkable visitor had. He wished now that he had spent every possible minute with him, and he grieved the loss of his presence.

David's feet kept hitting roots and fallen trees; branches kept getting into his face, but the anger in his gut was gone. He asked the Father to expand the peace growing in him.

Overhead, clouds had lessened, and stars were becoming slightly visible above the treetops. David tried to keep his eyes on them, and as he walked on and on, eventually he also saw what seemed like a flicker of light on ground level. Bending down and looking around trees, he tried to see it again. Soon he saw many flickers of light, like fireflies. A few more steps and he realized they were actually starlight or moonlight reflecting on waves. He was at last at the lake.

Relief surged through him like a runner's high, like achieving victory at a game. But it wasn't his victory, he thought; it was the victory of Michael's prayers. Nearing the lake, despite his exhaustion, he felt like leaping into the water and giving a great shout of deliverance.

He didn't. Instead he walked to water's edge. He could see the lights of the hotel across the lake. He wanted to go to the bench, hoping that Michael was there or somewhere nearby.

Most of the clouds had vanished, with only a few scattered low on the horizon. As he walked the perimeter of the lake toward the bench, David welcomed the sound of the frogs' throaty serenade resonating across the water. At his approach, bull-frogs splashed in one by one.

Halfway back, he could make out the bench. It was empty.

David kept walking until he got to the bench; then he gripped its back in his hands, looking in all directions. No Michael.

He sat down and scanned the shoreline. A half-moon cast a thin path of light on the lake, but David saw no movements. He swatted at a mosquito near his ear. Was Michael gone for good? Should he call out to him? He'd told David he couldn't stay long. Was this visitor who had flip-flopped his life even now "slipping through a membrane"?

A shooting star caught David's eye, and after a few moments, he noticed a pulsating satellite moving in its steady arc. He felt relieved after his ordeal and energized by his spiritual rebirth, but he also felt overwhelmed by the extraordinary day, and he began thinking of what it would be like tomorrow when he'd face all the problems that had made him slam off those alarms that morning. How would he integrate these incredible experiences?

Above him the moon was luminous among glittering stars. As he watched the thin ripple of its light across the dark expanse of the lake, he thought he caught a whiff of something.

What was it? Yes! A whiff of that wondrous fragrance. And at the same time he heard music—just a few notes and not very loud this time, but that same triumphant sound—and with it a brilliant flash of a vivid blue light. The light was so bright he squinted, and the stars and moon disappeared for a moment as if it were midday.

It was over before he could blink. The stars and moon reappeared.

He eased back on the bench, his eyes on the path of moonlight on the waves. He felt he had just received a farewell message. "Thank you, Michael," he whispered. "Thank you."

For long moments he pondered and savored the fact that he was likely the only one who had seen and experienced this coming and going between worlds. He felt a deep personal connection to Michael and wondered if this remarkable celestial being was now aware of his sitting on this bench listening to the waves lapping against the sand. Gratitude, wonderment, new determinations were all rising in him.

Another mosquito buzzed near his ear. His sweat had dried, but he was increasingly aware of the sting of his scraped neck and hands and the muddy bruises on his arms and legs. He needed a shower. In fact, as soon as he thought about it he felt a desperate need for one.

In his room he undressed, put the hotel shampoo and soap on the tub's edge, and stepped in. The water felt both cleansing and soothing. As he absently rubbed the soap, gratitude flowed over him like the warm water. He'd once read that gratitude is the healthiest emotion of all. He started expressing his gratitude to the Father above and found it calmed his anxieties and changed his perspectives. When he finally dried and stepped onto the bath mat, he marveled that such a short time ago he had been lost, but now he stood feeling secure in body and soul.

David was only half dressed when he spied the Bible Michael had left open on the table. He buttoned his shirt as he bent over the table to look at the words of Jesus that Michael had marked: "I have come as a light to shine in this dark world."

He saw other marked pages. "Don't let your hearts be troubled," Jesus had said just before His own death. "Trust in God, and trust also in me. There is more than enough room in my Father's home. . . . I am going to prepare a place for you."

David shook his head. *Do people know what's actually in the Bible?* Jesus was going to "slip through a membrane," and He called the place

He was going "home." He told His friends not to be afraid.

"Don't be afraid!" Angels had said it at Christmas, and so had Jesus. David saw that Jesus had also said, "I have loved you even as the Father has loved me. . . . When you obey my commandments, you remain in my love. . . . I have told you these things so that you will be filled with my joy."

Joy. Joy and gratitude. Both flowed in David's heart as he read. His doubts, his intellectual questions, his fears of losing his freedoms—all were swept away like words made of plastic on a little child's desk. The questions remained hard, but a gritty reality transcended them.

David kept reading the chapters in John's Gospel, in which Jesus, facing death, talked to His friends. "I came from the Father into the world, and now I will leave the world and return to the Father. . . . I am praying not only for these disciples, but also for all who will ever believe in me."

Did that mean David was now in Jesus' circle

of friends? He grabbed a highlighter and in bright green marked "for all who will ever believe in me."

"I believe," he said aloud. He was amazed that Jesus' words applied to him: "I have loved you even as the Father has loved me. Remain in my love."

David desperately wanted to remain in His love, but how?

"Just as you sent me into the world," Jesus had prayed to His Father, "I am sending them into the world."

What did that mean for him?

He threw himself on the bed and stared at the white ceiling. As never before in his life, he was fully aware of his weaknesses. Yet he could still see the fire in Michael's eyes when he'd said, "David, you are called."

In his extensive reading of biographies, certain men had captured David's imagination, and he had studied each of them in depth. Washington. Lee. Lincoln. MacArthur. Eisenhower. Great men all, and like all men, flawed. He thought about the tumultuous times and enormous challenges these men had faced and the ways they had earnestly sought divine guidance. Washington always invoked the blessing of Providence and, when blessings came, attributed them to God. Robert E. Lee's deep faith never wavered. Lincoln's spiritual growth was incredible. David once had stood in the Lincoln Memorial and slowly and repeatedly read his second inaugural address, etched into the marble.

Reading Lincoln's address as he stood not far from the sixteenth president's giant marble figure had said many things to David, among them that greatness comes from humility, and that God's purposes ultimately rule. Lincoln had a clear-eyed view of how heaven transcended earth.

Heaven. Earth.

Michael had made a strange comment: "The new heaven, the new earth starts with your soul."

New heaven and new earth? His soul? He knew Michael's descriptions of celestial wonders were far beyond his human imagination, and so was his comment about his soul. What new heaven and earth were to come, and how was he to prepare his soul?

A quote came to him from his reading of biographies: "Greatness starts in doing very small things exceptionally well." Small things. Respond to Jesus' love by obeying His commands.

Obey.

Obedience came hard. Very hard. Yet he realized small acts had enormous consequences.

David sensed that he needed to reach out to those two guys he couldn't stand.

He dreaded the idea. He had no desire to break from this sweet communion with the Father, Son, and Spirit he was experiencing in his room. He'd had enough trauma for one day, and he wanted to just pull the covers up over him and sleep. Yet he knew that this sweet communion had its demands.

Biting his upper lip, he put on his jacket and stepped outside. It was near midnight. Hopefully everyone had gone to bed.

However, as soon as he looked at the porch at the side of the lodge, he groaned inwardly. The moon and stars were still bright, and Pete and Ed were still on their rocking chairs.

David wanted to handle this in the morning, not now. He twisted a birch leaf between his fingers. He prayed for the Spirit to dissipate his anger toward these men.

As he prayed, he remembered Michael's enthusiastic comment: "David, you'll be amazed at how your prayers will be answered in ways you never could expect!"

David watched Pete and Ed rocking slowly back and forth, their old bodies sagging into the slats of the rockers. Looking at them, he felt something stirring in his heart. Was this the beginning of compassion?

As he kept praying, he was reminded of how it had been in college football. He dreaded getting crushed by huge linebackers, but the fear had morphed into energy and spirit. Obedience, he thought, was now morphing his fears into spirited resolve.

He forced himself to walk over to the two men, still dreading the encounter as he had the linebackers, but he was determined to listen and to obey.

Pete noticed him, stopped rocking, and eyed David.

"Good evening," David said. "Glorious night."

"You could say that." The voice was flat, almost digital.

"Not much glory in these mosquitoes," Ed said, scratching his bare leg.

"No," David replied. "But those stars and moon are glorious. The Creator puts on quite a show for us!"

The men looked at him quizzically, obviously taken aback at his warm spirit. Pete coughed.

Ed glanced at Pete. He cocked his head at David and looked up at the heavens. "Yeah. Quite a show."

David smiled at them both. Then he simply said, "Well, good night," and walked away.

He felt exhilarated. Such a small, small action, but not at all inconsequential. He had been obedient in that small thing. Michael had told him to stay in step with the Spirit. He felt he was in step—just a little step, but maybe lots of little steps would contribute to a new earth, whatever that might mean.

Midnight or not, mosquitoes or not, he wanted to go back to the bench and pray.

He sat under the wonder of the stars and listened to the movements of the water. First thing in the morning he would call Marcia. Intensely aware of his bent toward melancholia, he prayed he would keep alert to the Spirit. Michael had told him, "Remember what Jesus said. 'Ask, and you will receive.'"

He prayed for a very long time. He thought again and again of Michael's final words: "Listen. Listen for the music." That snatch of music when blue light had illumined the night sky kept playing in his soul, and he envisioned Michael moving rhythmically to it.

David watched the lake and listened. No supernatural music came, but he did hear music. The chords of Handel's *Messiah* reverberated in his mind. David loved classical music. He let the familiar chorus repeat several times, leaning back and listening, savoring the words. He mused on how perfectly *Messiah*'s majesty and joy matched his experience as he was coming out of the forest.

So much of earth's music is marvelous, he thought. So much creativity on earth transcended the corruption. Even a spider was magnificent!

He let other music go through his mind, Bach and Beethoven. He also hummed songs like the Beatles' "Eleanor Rigby" and "Lady Madonna," brilliant works calling for compassion and engagement.

Compassion and engagement. Handel and Bach inspired, he thought, but there was also the music of the oppressed in a world full of anguish. He firmly set his jaw. He could do so little in such a complex, troubled world. But if he kept listening, his little would be enough.

His hand grazed something beside him on the bench. He felt for the object and found nestled in a corner a neat stack of small stones. He ran his fingers over the edges. Flat. Three, carefully selected and perfect for skipping. Had Michael left them for him?

David was sure he had! He grabbed all three and strode to the water's edge.

Bending down, he gripped one stone with his thumb on top and his forefinger curled around its edge. He studied the ripples of water in the path of moonlight leading toward his feet and cocked his arm. Suddenly the full joy of determination and purpose surged through him. He felt his arm pulse with power as his body followed his arm's whiplike movement and the snap of his wrist that sent the stone flying.

The stone hit right where he had aimed, in the center of the moonlit path, and like a continuation of his arm's motion, it spanked the water so hard it lifted off just as Michael's had this morning. Though he couldn't see its trajectory, he was sure it had taken off like a bird in flight.

But only one stone. He felt the energy subside as he fingered the remaining two in his other hand. He bent again and with a snap of his wrist sent them low and hard just above the water. One skipped four times, the other seven.

Would he have a magnificent role to play, like Washington or Lincoln? It didn't matter—didn't matter at all! As Lincoln had said, God would bring about His own purposes. It would be with or without David.

A new heaven. A new earth. And here on earth, wasn't it Elizabeth Barrett Browning who wrote of "every common bush aflame" with glory if we but open our eyes?

He noticed something white far out above the lake. Slowly it grew larger, and he soon saw it was coming toward him. As it neared, he made out in the moonlight the graceful wings of a great white heron.

It kept flying toward him. The muted white of its body and wings contrasted with the brightness of the stars and moon and made the heron look to David like a heavenly apparition. Its wings in their steady movements made it seem to float in the starlight. As the great bird closed the gap between them, it soared almost directly above where he was standing.

Crack! Just as the heron was overhead, a loud sound like a shotgun blast made David flinch. He twisted around in alarm and anger, scanning the big lawn and lodge porch to see what had happened. He saw nothing and quickly looked back up at the heron. Unperturbed, it was sailing over the trees, flapping its silvery wings in its steady rhythm.

Had the sound come from a shotgun? Or had it come from revelers setting off a harmless cherry bomb? David eased onto the bench, figuring he'd never know. The white speck of the heron disappeared in the darkness, and he stared at the stars in the same patch of sky.

Unperturbed. He longed to be unperturbed like that heron, but he was still shaken. Taking a very deep breath, he slowly breathed out. He closed his eyes and sought to see again the white heron's wondrous appearance in the moonlight and its steady flight directly over him.

Slowly he opened his hands and lifted them a little. "Thank You," he whispered for the second time that evening. "Thank You."

About the Author

Harold Myra served as the CEO of Christianity Today International for thirty-two years. Under his leadership, the organization grew from one magazine to a communications company with a dozen magazines, copublished books, and a major Internet ministry.

Myra started his journalistic career with *Youth for Christ* magazine, which under his leadership became *Campus Life* magazine.

Author of five novels, numerous children's and nonfiction books, and hundreds of magazine articles, Myra has taught writing and publishing at the Graduate School of Wheaton College in Illinois. He holds honorary doctorates from several colleges, including Biola University in California and Gordon College in Massachusetts.

Myra has received various awards, among them the prestigious Magazine Publisher's Award and the James DeForest Murch Award from the National Association of Evangelicals. The Evangelical Press Association presented him with its highest honor, the Joseph T. Bayly Award, for his triple career as an editor, author, and publishing executive.

Harold and his wife, Jeanette, are the parents of six children and grandparents of five. They reside in Wheaton, Illinois.